Pirates

First published by William Collins Sons & Co Ltd in 1987
First published in Picture Lions in 1988
This edition published in 1992

Picture Lions is an imprint of the Children's Division,
part of HarperCollins Publishers Limited,
77-85 Fulham Palace Road, Hammersmith,
London W6 8JB

Printed in Great Britain

Pirates

by Colin and Jacqui Hawkins

PictureLions
An Imprint of HarperCollins Publishers

Pirate Spotting

Pirates are the scourge of the seven seas and the terror and dread of all honest sea-faring folk. These wicked and wily robbers, these outlaws of the oceans, are feared by friend and foe alike.

Never trust a pirate. Blink for a moment and they'll have the rings off your fingers and the bus pass from your purse. They will stop at nothing in their fierce quest for golden goodies and silver sparklies. These rum-reeking rogues will spit in your eye for a penny.

Can you recognise a pirate? Would you spot one in a crowd? If you have never seen a seadog read carefully this old pirate lore:

"Knows't a pirate by the hook on his arm, the parrot on his shoulder and the black patch on his eye. Or, 'arken to the thud clump, thud clump of his peg leg and crutch as he crosses ye olde tavern floor."

There may be a pirate in your area. Has anyone *you* know lost a parrot?

Pirates wear warm hardwearing clothes. Captains like to have big hats and jackets with large pockets for doubloons, cannon balls and maps. As they love to be noticed, they wear bright colours, lots of lace, gold buttons and gold trim.

Emergency Grog.

St Chistopher medals.

Knee length Nautical Knickers

Gob yer Shut!

Sea Sock (resistant to salt rot)

Pirate Personals

Pirates travel light. Crowded cabins and hoards of hammocks leave little room for pirate accessories. Life on board can be very squashed, so the modern buccaneer has few luxuries.

Locket of Loved ones

Boss

Mother

1st June 1726
Beans and rhubarb again for vittles. Keel Hauled the Cook

2nd June 1726
Didst Suffer much with the wind and the Squitters

Log
Every day diary of pirate folk.

Jolly Roger time piece.

Only wallies wash. Grubby pirates get clean in the sea when they fall in. No self-respecting pirate has a toothbrush – but rubs his gums and teeth (if he has any) in salt water. Long sea voyages make it difficult for those regular dental checkups, so pirates do not get the fillings they need. Pirates with problems pull out rotten teeth or spit them into the sea. Older sea rogues pride themselves on their toothless grins. It shows they've been around.

As it is a long way to the launderette, pirates do not wash their clothes. The combination of sea salt and grime adds that extra layer they need to keep out the cool sea breezes. Smelly seadogs freshen up with a splash of 'Eau de Channel'.

Pirates often lose bits of themselves in battle, so they always keep peg legs, hooks and eye patches handy.

Ha!Har!

Spare
Hook
and
cork screw
attachments

Eye patch.

eye eye Cap'n

Glass eye
and set of teeth
for Sunday best.

Ho Har!

Bug

Bug rake

Blackspot to be given to
land lubbers
and sissys.

'Black spot will make ée rot'
(Old pirate curse.)

Pirate Customs

Pirate crews always vote for their captain. This means anyone can be captain if they get enough votes. It is more fun being captain as you get the biggest share of the booty.

To be a successful captain you have to shout very loudly. Captains need to give orders out on deck. This can be a strain and many pirates suffer from sore throats. Some may even lose their voices completely. Do you know of anyone with a sore throat? Has your teacher ever lost her voice?

On long sea voyages pirates can pass the time playing games. You may know some of these:-

Musical Hammocks
Hunt the Grog
Pass the Cannonball
Kiss Chase
Sharks (Pirates' version of Sardines)
What's the time Cap'n Hook?
Snarl (Pirates' version of Snap)

Walking the plank is a popular method of disposing of an unwanted crew member.

New pirates sign "the pirate's charter" and swear on the Bible to be loyal and true crew members. Is there a Bible in your classroom?

Oh! Goodie it's dinner time!

I swear to be really really bad... and really really wicked... and...really really rude.. and...

Note use of three fingers!

Pirate food is very boring. Sea faring cooks are not usually very imaginative due to the fact that everything has gone off after a few days. Some pirate chefs, however, do have flair, and can improvise with the odd seaweed soufflé, grilled gull, poached parrot, or shark shurprise.

Har! Har!

A favourite treat is a sort of pirate muesli called Figgie Dowdie. This is a fruit pudding made with currants and raisins.

"Figgie Dowdie is our favourite pud,
We get it when we're very good."

Pirates mostly eat extremely hard biscuits called 'tack'. Unfortunately, horrible weevils and black spotted maggots like to burrow and live in these biscuits. Some pirates love maggoty tack, others dunk the biscuits in their grog to improve the flavour. Hence the word 'tacky'.

Grrrr!

Ancient pirate rhyme:-
"To eat hard tack
You need the knack
Or else yer pearlies you will crack!"

Bet 'ee 10 doubloons Blackie wins!

Yer on!

Pirate Pops

It is vital for a pirate ship to have a band on board. Singing and dancing are an important part of pirate therapy. A pirate who plays an instrument is much prized.

As evening draws in weary pirates blink blearily into the flickering lamplight, and hanging in hammocks, hum happily as the accordionist plays. Many a sea shanty can be heard wafting over the moonlit waves on a still night. Pirates need to unwind from sea stress.

Another function of the band is to play loudly as the pirates go into battle. The awful banging of the drums, the piercing screech of the violins and the yowling of the crew, strike terror into the hearts of the enemy.

We are ssssailin... &
We are sssailin... &
acrossss... the...
sssseq...

Isn't that a great song?

Grand.

Lovely.

The cat's good too.

Popular pirate tunes are:-

"Bailing Out"
"It's a Long Way to Tip a Sailor"
"We are Assailin'"
"You'll never Walk (the plank) Alone"
"Bad Booty Blues"

All at Sea

A pirate ship in full sail is a terrifying sight. It will send shivers to your spine and make your hair stand on end. Woe betide any God-fearing sailor when the dreaded skull and crossbones looms on the horizon.

In order to catch and plunder treasure galleons, pirate ships have to sail very quickly. This means they have a lot of sails and a large crew to man all the guns and keep the ships in good repair.

Crows nest
Where pirate crows
keep watch for ships
to plunder.

Pirate weather Lore

Blue patch in the
sky good weather
bye 'an bye.

Sun afore seven
storm afore eleven.

Gulls on the sail
watch out for
the gale.

Pirate loos are always
at the front of the ship on the
poop deck. This is close to the
figure head. Hence the rhymes

'Visit the 'ead'
fore ye go to bed'.
and 'Never in a gale put yer
bum o'er the rail'.

Pirate Ploys

Pirates love to play tricks. One favourite pirate prank is to sneak up on treasure ships. This they do by flying the flag of honest sea-faring folk, so they can sail up close. Then, at the last moment, the wily weasels hoist the Jolly Roger and hop aboard in a flash.

Another pirate trick is pretending to be ladies in distress. Unsuspecting, gallant sailors hasten to rescue these helpless damsels of the seas – only to feel the sharp point of a cutlass in their vitals. The sight of a great, hairy pirate in a bonnet and petticoat will haunt many an old sea salt to the end of his days.

Into Battle Ha Har

Pirates like nothing better than a good fight. The smell of gunpowder, the roar of cannons, the clash of steel on steel and the grappling of grappling hooks. All this is music to their ears.

A pirate has to be good at swinging from one ship to another. This has to be practised and crew members keep in trim with a daily searobics session.

Sometimes pirates prefer the captured ship to their own. So they swop them round. This is called Swopship.
Hence the well-known tongue-twister: 'He swops seaships on the seashore!'

Treasure Island

Pirates who collect lots of treasure like to bury it on deserted islands to keep it safe. Sometimes they draw maps to help them remember where they left it. As they do daft drawings and silly spelling pirates often cannot find the treasure when they return to dig it up. This means it is still waiting to be found.

Long ago the island of Tortuga was a hot favourite with pirates. Rumour has it that a huge hoard of treasure is still there, guarded by a giant tortoise called Tommy. Do you have a tortoise? It may well be a relation.

Pirate captains can be very greedy and take twice as much treasure as everyone else. Some captains (especially those with one eye) are not very good at counting, so they do not divide the spoils equally. This can make them unpopular with the crew!

In their search for buried treasure, pirates become enthusiastic diggers!

Pirates in Petticoats

Anne Bonney and Mary Read were notorious lady pirates of days gone by. These hellcats of the oceans were a fearsome pair, who struck terror in the hearts of their crew. They were particularly fierce if a pirate was not polite and forgot to say "please" and "thankyou".

Touch an air of me sweeties 'ed and I'll cut 'ee gizzards orf!

Ar!

Take yer at 'orf in the presence of a lady!

Many mums today like a spin on the high seas. Perhaps your mum is a lady pirate. Do you know of a mum with a frightening gaze and a hearty cry? – "Tidy your bunk! Ha, Har! Scrub yer teeth and clean yer 'ead!" does this sound like your mum? Does your mum dish up hard tack for tea?

Scurvey dog!

Aye

Pirate Who's Who

Eustace the Monk

A 12th century pirate known as the 'Black Monk'. People said he had magic powers and could make his ship invisible. It was certainly difficult to cross the Channel without giving him a donation.

Chin Yin and Hsi Kai

Two notorious Chinese pirates, who held a British crew hostage for a huge ransom. This cunning Eastern pair spotted the shiny, brass buttons on the officers' uniforms. Thinking they were gold, they naturally presumed the English navy was very rich. They were wong.

Olaf the Viking

One of the earliest pirates. This chap thought he was very funny, and his gruesome giggling and loony laughter warned enemies of his approach.

Ha! Har!

Ha! Har! Avast! an Belay! Ha! Har!

Will honourable gentleman give Yin and Kai lots of buttons?

Most Kind

Who's Who

Barbarossa (Redbeard)

This pest of a pirate plundered the coasts of France and Spain. Some people said that he dyed his beard with the blood of his enemies.

It's tomato ketchup really

mmm... tastes good.

Blackbeard →

Avast! and Belay! or I'll cut ee! gizzerds orf!

Whats a gizzerd?

Dunno!

Ali Pasha

An evil and vicious Eastern pirate who killed or enslaved Christians. People often thought he kept his treasure in his turban!

Ali Pasha is a smasha.

Blackbeard (Edward Teach)

One of the most fearsome looking pirates of all times. Blackbeard was extremely hairy, with an enormous black beard and hairy hands. His favourite trick was to go into battle with lighted tapers flaming in his beard.

Bartholomew Roberts

A very strict pirate who made all his crew members be in their hammocks by eight o'clock. On Sundays he read the Bible to his crew, and never drank anything other than tea.

Get to sleep ye scurvey knaves 'tis gorn eight bells.

And the Lord sayeth ...

Get to bed by 8'o'clock

Aye Aye cap'n

Yes Sir

can I have a drink of water.

Pirate Yarn

There once was an old sea dog
Who loved to drink plenty of grog

At the Mad Maggot's Bar
He told tales of afar
And of ships that got lost in the fog.

With his eye on a wench,
He'd sit on a bench
His yarns they were awfully scarey

Of terrible gales
Or 'orrid great whales
and creatures who looked very hairy!

"The places I've been
And the booty I've seen
You folks would not think it true."

"With cutlass and sword
We'd throw men overboard
And capture the captain and crew!"

At the end of the day
This pirate would say
that rovin' it gave him no pleasure,

But as the dawn broke
And the sea dog awoke,
He'd set sail to look for more treasure.
Ha Har!

At the end of every adventure pirates love to throw a party. Swilling much grog and munching burnt, black sausages, they dance and sing till dawn.

"Yo, ho, ho, and a bottle of rum,
A burnt, black sausage in my tum.
So put on your peg leg, yer eye-patch too,
If you're after treasure you can join our crew."